Halloween
AT SUNSHINE FARM

MaryLou Quillen

Published by Yellow Button Press. ISBN: 9798696118154

The kids at Sleepy Hollow school
Were finishing up their day
When Miss Gray received a message
Delivered in a special way

Inside was an invitation, with a special Halloween note
From Farmer Rick at Sunshine farm
And this is what he wrote:

"WE'RE HAVING A COSTUME CONTEST
AND A CORN MAZE HAS BEEN PREPARED
THERE'LL BE GAMES, TREATS AND A TROPHY
SO MAKE PLANS TO MEET US THERE!"

The kids rushed home to get ready
Each was hoping to be the best
To choose the perfect costume
That would win the Halloween Contest

That night they followed the scarecrows
Pointing the way to Sunshine farm
Where Farmer Rick placed bales of hay
Around two stages in the barn

The first to step up to the stage was a wee witch
shaking her broom

"Pick me or
I'll put a spell on you!"
She warned everyone
in the room

"Hold on," shouted a fearless knight
Who defeated dragons galore

"I am the one to
fear this night,
I'm winning this
contest for sure!"

Just then dark Dracula woke up
And swung wide open his cape

"You all must surrender to me,
From this, you cannot escape!"

Suddenly there was a thunderous thud
Everyone frantically looked around

A green monster
was stomping by
Making awful
gurgling sounds

"Ahoy, Maties, don't be alarmed
And don't shudder with such fright.
It's only Franky Frankenstein,
Argh, t'will be me
who wins tonight!"

"Not so fast," someone called out,
"I think you should consider me
I'm your neighborhood fireman
And I work hard for your safety!"

"Alas, dear friends, please step aside
For I am royalty, you see

I'm the fairest in
all the land
So, of course, you
must choose me!"

"I am here to save the day
This isn't a costume that I wear
I am really a Superman
Watch as I leap up in the air!"

Then the stage started spinning
Or so it seemed to Sid
For he was doing kicks and spins
Dressed as the Karate Kid

A future NASA pilot
(at least, that's what James
dreamed he'd be)
Stuck a perfect airplane landing
On the stage for all to see

Next came an allstar with a bat
Swinging at an invisible ball
He was sure his costume choice
Would be the one to beat them all

A dark robed figure stood very still
Then slowly walked into the light

"If I use my Jedi
mind trick,
you will name me
the winner tonight!"

"Wait for me," a baker called out
"I'm running a little late,
I wanted to do something special
So I baked Halloween cupcakes!"

Even the teacher stepped on stage
Miss Gray dressed as a leprechaun

She held her lucky
green clover
As she joined in
the Halloween fun

Then came the final contestant
A silly clown who was all the rage

Everyone roared with laughter...

When
Silly Jilly
took the stage!

The decision was unanimous
Jilly won the Halloween contest
For being the 'Most Original'
Her costume was voted the best!

And when the party was over
The kids gave Jilly a roaring cheer
They pledged to return to Sunshine farm
To see who would win the prize next year!

Now it's time to choose YOUR costume
It can be old, new or in between
Because as silly Jilly would tell you (if she could talk)
Dressing up is the best part of Halloween!

Happy Halloween to all the
trick-or-treaters out there!

If you enjoyed this book, please leave a review. Thank you!

This book belongs to:

Note to parents and carers

Many children are now taught to read using the phonic approach. This means they are taught to look at the letters, say the sounds, and then blend them to make a word. So, for example, children blend **c/a/t** to make the word **cat**, and **sh/o/p** to make **shop**.

When children have completed their initial phonics learning, they are ready to apply it to reading real books. Ladybird's **Superhero Phonic Readers** are planned for this exciting stage.

Some words are hard to read using beginner phonics. These words are often known as 'tricky words'. Some of these occur frequently in the English language so it is useful for children to memorize them.

Have fun doing our Tricky Words Memory Quiz on page 30. This features the most useful tricky words from the story.

How to use Superhero Phonic Readers:

- ★ Start at level one and gradually progress through the series. Each story is a little bit longer than the last and uses more grown-up vocabulary.
- ★ Children will be able to read **Superhero Phonic Readers** for themselves. Let your child read to you, and share the excitement!
- ★ If your child finds any words difficult, help him or her to work out the sounds in the word.
- ★ Early readers can be concentrating so hard on the words that they sometimes don't fully grasp the overall meaning of what they read. The puzzle questions on pages 28 and 29 will help with this. Have fun talking about them together.
- ★ There is a reward chart at the back of the book - young readers can fill this in and add stickers to it.
- ★ The Ladybird website **www.ladybird.com** features a wealth of information about phonics and reading.
- ★ Enjoy reading together!

Geraldine Taylor
Ladybird Educational Consultant

Educational Consultant: Geraldine Taylor

Phonics Consultant: Marj Newbury

A catalogue record for this book is available from the British Library

Published by Ladybird Books Ltd
80 Strand, London, WC2R 0RL
A Penguin Company

2 4 6 8 10 9 7 5 3 1
© LADYBIRD BOOKS LTD MMIX
LADYBIRD and the device of a Ladybird are trademarks of Ladybird Books Ltd

ISBN: 978-1-40930-262-9

Printed in Italy

Superhero
Phonic Readers

X-Ray Rex

written by Mandy Ross

illustrated by Mark Ruffle

Things kept going missing at Zoobody Zoo.
Mrs Zoobody, the boss, had lost her ring and her keys.

Tiger Tim had lost his keeper, Kim.
And seven penguins were missing.
"What shall I do?" said Mrs Zoobody.

"Can I help?" said X-Ray Rex.
X-Ray Rex has x-ray eyes. He can use
x-ray beams to look right through things.

X-Ray Rex took a good look around.

Zoobody Zoo

"The ring is inside the snake," said X-Ray Rex.
"Tut, tut, Hissy," tutted Mrs Zoobody.
"The keys are inside the elephant,
and Keeper Kim is inside Tiger Tim."

"My goodness!" said Mrs Zoobody. "Quick!"

"Well done, X-Ray Rex," said Mrs Zoobody.
"Next, you must look for the penguins.
One has been going missing every day."

"Hmmm," said X-Ray Rex, and he sat down by the zoo gate to watch.

Soon, X-Ray Rex spotted a man with a cold face and a big bag. He x-rayed the bag.
"Aha!" said X-Ray Rex. "Baron Frostbite!"

"I will follow him," said X-Ray Rex.
"Take Hissy," said Mrs Zoobody.
"She can help you."

X-Ray Rex and Hissy followed Baron Frostbite.
He slipped through a small gate. X-Ray Rex
x-rayed the gate. He saw ice and penguins.

X-Ray Rex opened the gate.

"Welcome to my ice garden," cackled Baron Frostbite.

X-Ray Rex quickly looked around.
He x-rayed the blocks of ice. He saw people!

He x-rayed Baron Frostbite.
Something was hidden under his cloak.

"Look, Hissy!" said X-Ray Rex.
"It's an ice-zapper! He wants to turn us to ice!"

"Soon I will turn the world to ice!" cackled
Baron Frostbite, pointing the ice-zapper at X-Ray Rex.

"Not so fast!" said X-Ray Rex.
"Get him, Hissy!"

As quick as a flash, Hissy tied up Baron Frostbite.

X-Ray Rex grabbed the ice-zapper. He switched
it to 'melt'. He quickly zapped the blocks of ice.
"Thank you, X-Ray Rex," said the frozen people,
as the ice melted. "You saved us!"

The police took Baron Frostbite away to jail. "And now," said X-Ray Rex, "Hissy and the penguins need to get home."

"Welcome back!" everyone at the zoo cheered.
"Well done, X-Ray Rex!"

"You are a superhero, X-Ray Rex," said Mrs Zoobody. "Just one more thing. What about my keys, and my ring?"

"Oh dear," said X-Ray Rex. "You will just have to wait…!"

Superhero Secret Puzzles

⭐ What had Mrs Zoobody lost?

⭐ Where did X-Ray Rex find Keeper Kim?

⭐ What did Baron Frostbite want to do?

⭐ What kind of zapper did Baron Frostbite have?

⭐ How did X-Ray Rex stop Baron Frostbite from zapping him?

⭐ Would you like to have x-ray eyes?

Look at these pictures from the story and say the order they should go in.

A

B

C

D

Tricky Words Memory Quiz

Can you remember these words from the story?

See if you can read them super-fast.

going	he	wants
Mrs	to	so
the	through	oh
her	are	have
keys	my	
were	you	
what	one	
I	she	
do	people	
said	something	
eyes	was	

What else can you remember?

Can you put the book down and say what happens in the story?

The answer to the picture puzzle on page 29 is: D, A, B, C.

I'm a phonic

Superhero

I can read all of **X-Ray Rex**.

Well done!

I'm a reading hero

I can read all the tricky words.

By _____

Date _____

level 5

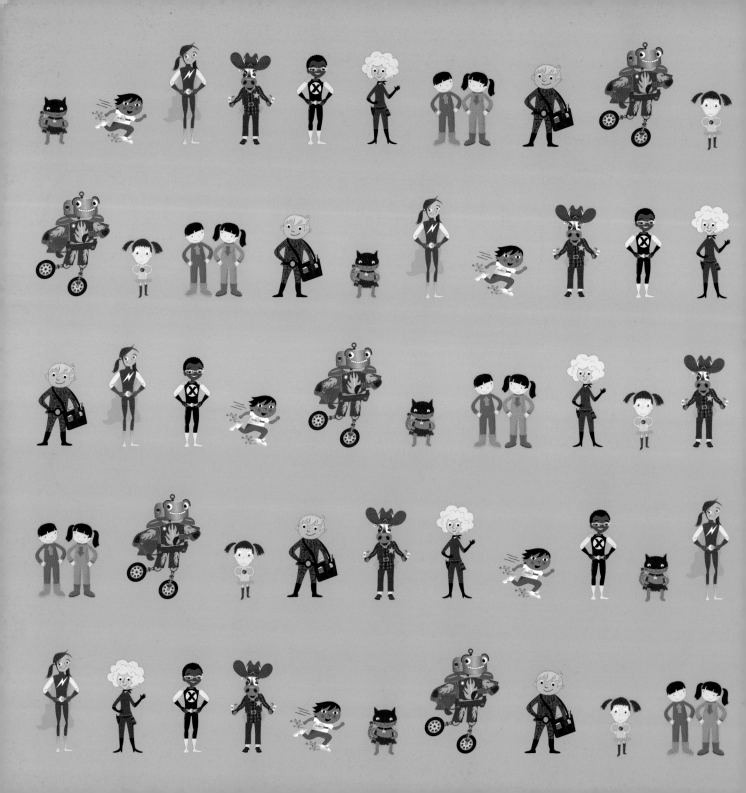